I knew that I had to
·me my arms, I need€
secrets of Willow Creek Harvest this is the
most traumatizing and haunting
incident of my life which cost me not only
my friends brother and both my arms but
also my sanity.

We were a group of four friends me and
my twin brother Sam, my best friend Ana
and William who was married to Sasha we
used to call him Will.

We graduated college together and
recently met at a class reunion where Will
introduced us to his work partner Nate
Nate was handsome and funny I was
immediately drawn to him, icy blue eyes
and curly brown hair he kept on cracking
jokes and entertaining everyone I couldn't
help but notice him sneak glances at me
which I found cute because I was

obsessing over him I confided in Ana that I wanted to get to know him better and she too observed the chemistry between us.

As we were leaving the gathering, Nate approached me and asked shyly for my phone number he expressed his interest in being friends with me without hesitation I handed him my phone so he could enter his number it was then that I noticed the tattoo on both his wrists two axes in a cross I didn't think much of it and actually found it quite cool.

That night, Nate texted me and shared more about himself he was originally from a small town in Russia and visited every spring for a harvest festival Despite being in LA for work, he expressed a desire to return to his hometown for the festival that year.

Curious, I asked him if he had a girlfriend, to which he denied having one I felt relieved and excited that we were getting closer we began texting constantly day and night and it soon became a part of our daily routine.

A few weeks later, Will and his wife Sasha invited us to their welcoming party, and to my delight, Nate was there too Ana kept nudging me to sit with him, and I couldn't help but feel overjoyed.

During lunch, Nate shared exciting news that he was planning to visit his hometown for the spring harvest festival and would love to take friends with him as he showed us pictures of his small town, we were awestruck by the beautiful lush green meadows, the quaint homes, and the breath taking fields of red spider lilies We all agreed to book a tour together, except for Will and Sasha, who were expecting a baby.

The next day, I excitedly packed my bags and informed my office about my leave I was determined to turn my friendship with Nate into a relationship and looked forward to the trip.

As I was packing, Sam entered my room and expressed his concerns about the tour. He wasn't sure if we should go since we didn't have any relatives in Russia, and we might lose internet access in the small town this worried him, as it could be problematic if we needed help in case of an emergency.

I brushed off Sam's worries, telling him not to be so paranoid Sam had always been overly cautious and would often warn me about potential dangers, but I never took his concerns seriously Despite his fears, I remained excited about the trip and confident that everything would be fine.

Finally, the day of the tour arrived. I wore my comfy sweats and got ready to go to the airport with Sam. We took Ana from her house in the cab and hurried our way to catch the flight. On the airport we were greeted by Nate.

He looked handsome and glorious as always throughout our flight I kept on secretly watching Nate and crushing on him we were given lunch within two hours of the flight which I devoured with delight.

Ana was sitting with me, and we watched movies and snuggled to sleep at night in the middle of the night I woke up and saw that the entire plane's lights were dim and almost everyone was sleeping and drowsing off except for Nate, he was staring at me.

I felt a bit uncomfortable with his gaze but soon settled down. I asked him if he's okay to which he gently smiled and said he was fine.

The following morning, our plane touched down at our destination Russia with excitement buzzing through us, we chatted our way out of the airport and onto the curb, where a car was already waiting for us Nate informed us that the driver was from his hometown, and we piled into the car to make our way there.

As we drove through the Russian countryside, taking in the stunning scenery, Nate regaled us with stories about his hometown we couldn't wait to see it for ourselves.

After a long and picturesque drive through the Russian countryside, the car eventually came to a halt at the entrance gate of Nate's hometown. The gate was marked with a sign that read "Willow Creek," accompanied by a symbol of two crossed axes.

With Nate as our guide, we passed through the gate and into the town itself as we walked along the main street, we were struck by the quaint charm of the place. Walking towards the outskirts of town, we came across a peculiar sight, long fields of wheat and corn were spread as far as the eye could see but between them was a field of red spider lilies.

The vibrant blooms were in full display, creating a breath-taking sea of red in between the fields that looked like sand.

I found this arrangement very odd but aesthetic at the same time, so I asked Nate why were the fields surrounding the spider lily field and what these symbolize to which he told me that it's a traditional thing.

Every year after the harvest ritual in the town, the spider lily field grows flowers in remembrance of the people that passed away. I found that touching however Sam asked him about the people who were sacrificed to which Nate kept quiet.

As we continued our stroll around the outskirts of Willow Creek, our group stumbled upon a strange and intriguing sight. In the distance, we saw a collection of huts, each seemingly built from different materials and haphazardly placed around a larger, central wooden building.

We were immediately drawn to this unusual arrangement and made our way over to get a closer look as we approached, we could see that the huts were all constructed in a variety of styles, with some made of wood, others of stone, and still others of thatch.

Despite their differences, all the huts seemed to be arranged in a circular pattern around the central building, almost as if forming a protective ring around it.

The wooden building at the centre was particularly impressive, with intricate carvings and a large front door that seemed to beckon us inside we couldn't help but feel a sense of mystery and intrigue as we gazed at the unusual sight before us.

All of the town's people had congregated in a large open ground beside their huts, working together to prepare for an upcoming festival the air was filled with cheerful singing, laughter, and the sounds of wood being chopped, and food being cooked in large pots.

The men were dressed in brown waistcoats over loose white shirts and trousers, while the women wore plain white gowns with matching brown waistcoats. The young girls, on the other hand, had opted for a belt on their gowns instead of a waistcoat.

Nate urged us to hurry and get dressed for the festivities. Some friendly girls led us to a hut where they gave us our new clothes and instructed us to change into them.

The wooden hut stood as a cozy retreat, offering a small room adorned with four neatly arranged beds and an open shelf to store our belongings alongside, a delicate, small shelf proudly displayed a vase adorned with a solitary red spider lily. In haste, we swiftly changed our attire, eager to join the vibrant gathering of townspeople.

As we stepped outside Nate took us to a beautifully decorated ground, the open area sprawled before us, a spacious expanse meticulously prepared to cater to the audience's enjoyment of the upcoming show.

As far as the eye could see, there was an

abundance of comfortable seating, arranged in perfectly aligned rows, providing unobstructed views of the captivating spectacle that awaited.

The gentle breeze whispered through the air, carrying with it the smell of food and earth. Nate sat beside me and told me I looked heavenly I blushed by his praise.

Sam and Ana sat on the row below me I noticed Sam getting anxious and Ana held his hand to comfort him.

I asked Nate what the festival was about to which he explained me that every year before harvesting season the town holds a special festival called "**Vesennva**" which means spring sacrifice.

The resonating sound of horns filled the

air, signalling the start of the event, and the seats quickly filled with a vibrant crowd. Positioned prominently at the forefront were two exquisite antique chairs, reserved for an elderly couple.

With utmost care and tenderness, a pair of girls guided an old woman to her seat, ensuring her comfort. Simultaneously, a group of young boys escorted an elderly man to the adjacent chair, offering their support.

As soon as they were settled, a triumphant blast from the horn marked the commencement of the proceedings the show started with a group of young girls and boys singing a unique and weird song in Russian, but Nate called it a folklore however it seemed quiet mysterious since the group was dressed in striking red robe and holding a red spider lily while chanting the song.

They then drew an inverted star on the ground, suddenly a woman appeared from a hut with an infant wrapped in a cloth.

She placed the infant in the star and began chanting some words while her body began to shiver, her eyes were quivering, and she looked like she was possessed. I was getting uneasy and wanted to go and help the woman, but Nate held my hand asked me to just watch.

The air reverberated with the woman's piercing cry, "O Ceres! accept this child of earth!" Instantly, the group of young boys and girls encircled the infant on the ground, their voices intertwining with the rhythmic throb of a drum.

The chant of "**O Ceres**" echoed passionately through the gathering, invoking the presence of a power.

As the drum's cadence reached its zenith, the group abruptly halted, each one clutching a pocketknife In a surreal moment, blades glinted in unison as they descended upon the infant the infant was stabbed by each one of the kids as he bled to death.

Sam, Ana, and I recoiled in horror, our voices erupting into screams at the harrowing sight of the infant being subjected to such torment yet, the surrounding crowd swiftly silenced us with disapproving glances and stern gestures. Suddenly, a woman rushed forward, bearing a drink in her hands.

Without questioning, we consumed it hastily, unaware of its effects. In no time, a wave of dizziness washed over me, pulling me into a profound slumber from which I could not resist.

As we gradually awakened, we found ourselves seated at the table, disoriented, and bewildered. To our astonishment, the farm was now filled with an atmosphere of mirth and jubilation and conversation intermingled with the clinking of glasses and the delightful aroma of sumptuous food.

It was a surreal transformation. The same people who had witnessed the shocking. event before now was revelling in the feast, indulging in the delectable fare spread before them we exchanged puzzled glances, trying to comprehend the inexplicable shift in the scene that unfolded before our eyes.

Nate, noticing my awakening, approached me with a glass of vibrant purple juice in his hand. Confusion clouded my mind as I struggled to comprehend the events that had unfolded.

With urgency, I questioned him about the unsettling act of sacrificing the infant and sought to understand the true purpose of this festival Nate, wearing a nonchalant expression, responded, "Hey, it's not a big deal, trust me.

By the way, did you notice the ring on your finger?" Startled, I glanced down to find a gleaming ruby ring adorning my hand. Bewildered, I attempted to remove it, but Nate swiftly interjected, "Baby, you can't alter your fate now It's the decree of Ceres that we must be united as husband and wife this harvest season.

Before I could process this bewildering information, Sam jolted me from my thoughts, urgently drawing my attention to my wrists to my horror, I discovered matching axe tattoos etched upon them. The sight left me speechless, grappling with a growing sense of unease and apprehension.

In the midst of my anguish and confusion, I mustered the courage to confront Nate about the haunting tattoos on our wrists.

Trembling with trepidation, I implored him, "Nate, what do these tattoos mean? Why are they necessary for this festival?" His gaze hardened, betraying the weight of tradition and the significance of our role.

With a solemn tone, Nate responded, "Jade, these tattoos symbolize our commitment to the sacred ritual they are a mark of our devotion to the ancient customs associated with this festival. They serve as a visible reminder of our intertwined destinies and the price we must pay for the blessings of the harvest It is a solemn duty, one that has been passed down through generations."

His words sent a chill down my spine, accentuating the gravity of the situation I struggled to reconcile the horror of the infant's sacrifice, the forced union between Nate and me, and now the indelible tattoos etched onto our flesh.

The weight of tradition pressed upon me,

and I felt the world around me morph into a dark, unfamiliar realm where the boundaries between ritual and reality blurred.

Though my heart longed for an escape from this twisted fate, Nate's unwavering conviction and the weight of tradition left me grappling with a harrowing truth that there might be no way to evade the grasp of this malevolent festival.

As uncertainty enveloped my mind, I began to question whether we could find a glimmer of hope within the shadows or if we were destined to be forever entangled in this macabre dance of sacrifice and devotion.

As the evening unfolded and the feast concluded, we were led back to our humble hut Ana and Sam, driven by desperation and the flickering ember of hope, hatched a daring plan to escape under the cover of darkness.

Whispers filled the air as we cautiously discussed our risky endeavour, fully aware of the peril that awaited us should we be caught Though their determination as palpable, a voice of caution.

Echoed within me. The thought of the unknown dangers lurking beyond the confines of this enigmatic town sent shivers down my spine I understood the stakes, the potential loss of life should our escape be discovered.

Yet, the oppressive weight of this twisted festival and the specter of our forced roles gnawed at my soul, driving me to consider the treacherous path my friends were determined to tread.

With trepidation and a glimmer of reluctant courage, we settled into a restless sleep, waiting for the opportune moment to flee.

It was decided that we would rouse ourselves from slumber when the entire town was submerged in the depths of their dreams, hoping to exploit the veil of night for our daring escape.

In the hushed stillness of the night, my eyes flickered open to find Ana silently awakening, her movements careful and deliberate curiosity mingled with apprehension, compelling me to abandon the safety of our shared slumber and trail after her as she stealthily made her way out of the hunt.

I saw in the cloak of darkness, Ana's silhouette flitted ahead, leading me through the maze of huts towards the towering edifice that stood at the heart of the town.

My heart pounded within my chest, the urgency of our escape melding with a gnawing sense of unease what could possibly draw Ana to this foreboding structure.

With each step, the shadows seemed to grow deeper, engulfing us in an eerie embrace. We approached the imposing building, its silhouette looming ominously against the night sky my pulse quickened, fuelled by a mixture of anticipation and trepidation, as Ana pushed open the creaking door and slipped inside.

I followed suit, the air heavy with anticipation and the scent of ancient secrets inside, an ethereal glow bathed the chamber, illuminating a scene that left me breathless.

The room pulsed with whispered incantations and the flickering light of candles a circle of individuals, cloaked in dark robes, encircled an altar adorned with symbols of Ceres. They were reading a book with an inverted star on the cover.

Suddenly a shadowy figure emerged from the depths of the building, seizing Ana with a force that sent her piercing screams reverberating through the chamber panic surged within me, an instinctual urge to rush her aid But before I could even take a step, Nate materialized beside me, his grip firm yet gentle, holding me back from the impending danger.

"Jade, don't go after her," Nate pleaded, his voice tinged with a mix of urgency and caution. "She came for this herself so it's time to accept her fate.

Confusion and fear entwined within me as I struggled against Nate's restraining grasp. The words echoed in my mind, leaving me torn between concern for Ana's well being and the enigmatic realization that she had sought answers within the depths of this foreboding building.

Questions swirled in my thoughts, demanding answers that remained tantalizingly out of reach. As I tried to resist Nate's grasp a needle was injected in my shoulder leading me to sleep

As I awakened, my face dampened by beads of sweat, I was gripped by an overwhelming sense of unease the remnants of a haunting nightmare clung to my thoughts, a chilling vision of Ana's demise It was as if the fabric of my dreams had woven together the darkest fears that lurked within my subconscious.

To my dismay, Sam sat beside me, tears streaming down his face, his expression a mirror of profound grief the sight sent a chill through my veins, and I trembled as I mustered the strength to ask him what had transpired. His voice quivered with sorrow as he whispered that Ana was dead.

Seeking answers, I implored Sam to explain, to shed light on this heart wrenching revelation. In response, he gestured towards the vase with a trembling hand, directing my attention to the single red spider lily it contained.

I asked him what is wrong, and he told me that Ana is dead, I asked him how he knows that to which he pointed at the red spider lily in the vase. "You didn't notice it but the first thing I saw when we entered this room is that the flower had only three petals and now one of the petals is gone that means Ana is dead."

Grief took over me as I tried to accept that Ana, my dear friend, had been taken from us, leaving behind an irreplaceable void that no words could adequately convey.

In the depths of my anguish, a fire ignited within me, an unyielding determination to escape the clutches of this wretched town and the insidious web of its rituals tears still streaming down my face, I resolved to play the role of a compliant lover, masking my true emotions behind a facade of affection and subservience.

As Nate approached my hut that day, I summoned a deceptive sweetness, embracing him with a kiss that belied the storm of hatred brewing within whispering words of adoration, I played the part of a grateful fiancée, echoing his belief that our union was a stroke of fortune.

Nate, taken aback by my sudden change in demeanor, expressed his surprise at my newfound compliance. he spoke of the impending harvest, emphasizing that our marriage would follow in its wake.

In that moment, I realized the urgency of

my mission to gather as much information as possible, to study the routines and movements of the townspeople, and to discern any potential vulnerabilities that might aid in our escape.

Throughout the day, I observed Nate's every action, scrutinizing his interactions with the others, noting the patterns and rituals that dictated their lives each moment spent by his side was a precious opportunity to glean insights, to uncover the secrets that bound this town and its people.

Nate took me to his favourite place in the town the Willow Creek Museum, he called it a sacred space that held the profound history of his town, along with its yearly harvest journal.

The room pulsated with an aura of mystique as my eyes landed upon vivid depictions of a young girl giving birth to a baby that bore an eerie resemblance to a demonic entity. The unsettling imagery evoked a sense of dread, as if peering into the depths of a dark, otherworldly realm.

The walls were adorned with intricate drawings portraying sinister figures associated with satanic lore, their forms accentuated by meticulously inscribed chants encircling them.

Among these macabre illustrations, one particularly harrowing image caught my attention, a pair of severed hands, blood cascading from their mutilated stumps. Etched onto the wrists were tattoos depicting axes, adding to the scene's gruesome symbolism.

Centered on the wall, a framed picture commanded my gaze. Closer examination revealed the aged countenance of the old man and woman, unmistakably the town's founders. The inscription "Founders" adorned the frame, cementing their significance Puzzling over the implications, I delved into extensive research, uncovering a disquieting truth that connected the pieces of this sinister puzzle.

It became apparent that our seemingly quaint town harboured a deeply ingrained cult, its leaders embodied by the old man and woman in the picture. Their practices centered around a ritualistic devotion to a malevolent entity named Ceres, evident from the references in the harvest journal and the haunting imagery within the sacred space.

The unnerving presence of the red spider lilies served as a crucial link to their sinister machinations, their symbolism intertwining with the cult's dark purpose.

Faced with this revelation, a chilling realization took hold our idyllic community was a facade, concealing a deeply rooted cult operating under the guide of normalcy.

The town's history, entwined with the founders' malevolent pursuits, hinted at a disturbing legacy that had thrived in secrecy for generations the significance of the ritual, the twisted depictions, and the haunting presence of the red spider lilies painted a grim portrait of a town entangled in an unholy covenant with darkness.

That night, after dinner, when Nate was heavily intoxicated, I mustered the courage to inquire about what had transpired on the evening Ana entered the foreboding building. Nate, with a somber expression, responded by promising to reveal the truth to me Intrigued and slightly apprehensive, I trailed behind him as we made our way to the ominous structure.

Upon entering, darkness enveloped us, rendering visibility scarce Illuminating our path with a flickering candle, Nate led me deeper into the shadows.

Suddenly my eyes fixated on an eerie sight a woman's figure captured within a display It was Ana, or at least a hauntingly distorted version of her there was an unsettling aura about her presence that sent shivers down my spine.

Compelled to investigate further, I cautiously approached the lifeless form, extending a trembling hand to touch her. As my fingertips made contact, an overwhelming surge of horror coursed through my veins.

I recoiled in sheer terror, for what I had touched was not Ana herself but a macabre imitation of her body It appeared as though they had taken her lifeless form and subjected it to the cruel practice of taxidermy.

To intensify the disquieting scene, two vibrant red spider lilies had been callously inserted into the empty sockets that once held Ana's eyes their contrasting hues stood out against the pallor of her face, serving as a grotesque reminder of the desecration inflicted upon her once-living form.

Overwhelmed by the shock of witnessing the horrifying fate that befell Ana, my anger towards Nate grew even more intense.

His twisted proclamation, referring to Ana as heroic for sacrificing herself in the name of the harvesting ritual, filled me with a profound sense of resentment. In that moment, a burning desire to escape this abominable town consumed me, and my thoughts turned to my twin brother, Sam.

Under cover of darkness, I carefully formulated a plan for our escape I knew that during the harvest, when the town would be preoccupied and engrossed in their malevolent practices, we would have a fleeting opportunity to steal the car parked by the barn it was our ticket to freedom, a chance to flee this nightmarish existence that had claimed the lives of so many.

With determination etched into my every thought, I shared the details of our plan with Sam that night we would wait for the chaotic flurry of activity that would inevitably consume the town during the harvest, then seize the moment to snatch the keys and make a swift getaway.

Our hearts pounding with anticipation, we would drive as fast as we possibly could, propelled by the desperate yearning to leave this accursed place behind.

Every aspect of our escape was meticulously calculated, from timing our departure to ensuring we had a clear path ahead.

We would leave no trace of our intentions, aiming to slip away unnoticed in the midst of the town's unholy revelry. The weight of our decision was heavy, for it meant severing ties with everything we had ever known, but the allure of liberation outweighed the fear of the unknown.

As the morning sun rose higher in the sky, enveloping the fields in its warm embrace, the town's inhabitants assembled for the harvest Nate, consumed by his duties, busily wielded his scythe to cut down the swaying wheat crops, while Sam dutifully aided him in the task meanwhile, I found myself amongst the group of girls, diligently picking ripe corn from the bountiful fields.

As time passed, the laborious work took its toll, and the collective weariness of the townsfolk prompted a well deserved break for lunch sensing our opportunity, Sam and I seized the moment to execute our escape plan. Swiftly, we retreated to our humble hut, ensuring no prying eyes followed our path.

Inside, we shed our worn work clothes, exchanging them for fresh garments that symbolized the beginning of our freedom. However, amidst the flurry of preparations, a glimmer of movement caught my attention in the periphery of my vision. Turning my gaze, I discovered that the red spider lily, once boasting two vibrant petals, now possessed only a solitary petal clinging to its delicate form.

We frantically made our way to the car, desperation fuelling our every move my heart raced as I noticed that it was an automatic vehicle, easing the burden of the impending escape without hesitation, we huddled inside, Sam taking the driver's seat, his hands trembling with anticipation. The engine roared to life, a glimmer of hope materializing before us.

But our moment of respite was shattered in an instant a menacing gang of townspeople, armed with axes and blades, descended upon us in a vengeful frenzy panic welled up within me, and I screamed at Sam to drive, to evade their clutches however, before we could make our escape, a man swiftly approached the car, wrenching open the door and forcibly dragging Sam out.

Helplessly, I watched in horror as he was subjected to a merciless beating, the sound of each blow echoing through the air. Nate, his face contorted with sadistic pleasure, seized the opportunity to assert his dominance.

He yanked me out of the car by my hair, a cruel smirk etched upon his lips spitting in my face, he delivered his chilling ultimatum, taunting me with a twisted proposition that would have spared my brother's life but the fire of defiance burned within me, refusing to succumb to his perverse desires.

With a grip that left me powerless, Nate dragged me towards a nearby log the world blurred through my tear-filled eyes as he raised his weapon, the sickening whoosh of the axe slicing through the air.

Agony engulfed me as the blade met my wrists, severing my hands in a horrifying act of retribution pain erupted within me, mingling with my anguished cries, as blood spurted from the raw wounds.

In the midst of the chaos, Sam fought against his captor, summoning every ounce of strength to break free with a defiant act of survival, he bit down on the hand restraining him, causing his captor to release his grip. In a desperate bid to ensure my escape, Sam propelled me into the car, his final words imploring me to flee at all costs.

As the car began to move, I witnessed the unfathomable horror unfold through the rear view mirror, Sam's life extinguished by the ruthless swing of an axe, his head severed from his body. Drenched in despair and exhaustion, I embarked on a harrowing journey, the car carrying me to another city in Russia where it stopped outside a hospital.

Weary and disoriented, I tumbled out of

the vehicle, met with the urgent attention of nurses who rushed to my aid the ensuing moments became a blur, my consciousness faltering as the gravity of my ordeal caught up with me, fading into the merciful respite of unconsciousness.

Eight long years have passed since that wretched chapter of my life, and justice has finally caught up with the malevolent inhabitants of the town I mustered the courage to report the horrifying truth I had witnessed to the authorities, and as a result, the town's sinister secrets were laid bare.

The once-thriving community became a desolate prison, its walls confining the likes of Nate and his accomplices the revelations that came to light were beyond comprehension. It was uncovered that the townspeople, under the guise of their harvest festival, were actually worshiping the demon known as Ceres.

They would entice unsuspecting individuals from around the world, drawing them into their clutches, only to sacrifice them in a twisted exchange for abundant crops and material wealth bestowed upon them by Ceres. Their ritualistic practices were steeped in darkness and depravity.

Outsiders, often women, were brought in as brides, with the intention of impregnating them and sacrificing their newborn babies. These innocent lives were callously buried in the red spider lily field, their blood offering awakening the slumbering powers of ceres, granting the cultists their ill-gotten review.

The extent of their heinous acts shook the foundation of justice and morality with the town shut down and its sinister underbelly exposed, the prisoners faced the consequences of their wicked deeds.

The perpetrators of these abhorrent crimes against humanity were held captive, their reign of terror forever halted. Though justice had prevailed, the scars of those dark years lingered within the survivors.

The memories of the sacrifices, the torment inflicted upon the innocent, and the twisted worship of a demonic entity haunted the minds of those who had managed to escape Healing would take time, but the revelation and closure brought a semblance of solace to the victims who had borne witness to the depths of human depravity.

As the town lay in ruins, it served as a chilling reminder of the darkness that can reside in the hearts of men but it also stood as a testament to the power of resilience and the determination to expose the truth the once fertile fields, tainted by bloodshed and sacrilege, now stood as a silent testament to the horrors that had transpired within those boundaries.

In the wake of this horrific revelation, steps were taken to ensure that such atrocities would never be allowed to resurface the tale of the town's descent into darkness became a cautionary tale, a chilling reminder of the depths to which humanity can sink when consumed by malevolence and fanaticism.

Printed in Great Britain
by Amazon

26115098R00026